SCRAPS

)6

For Sam

Copyright © 1990 by Mark Foreman.
This paperback edition first published in 2001 by Andersen Press Ltd.
The rights of Mark Foreman to be identified as the author and illustrator of this work have
been asserted by him in accordance with the Copyright, Designs and Patents Act, 1988.
First published in Great Britain in 1990 by Andersen Press Ltd.,
20 Vauxhall Bridge Road, London SW1V 2SA. Published in Australia by Random House Australia Pty.,
20 Alfred Street, Milsons Point, Sydney, NSW 2061. All rights reserved.
Colour separated in Switzerland by Photolitho AG, Gossau, Zürich.
Printed and bound in Italy by Grafiche AZ, Verona.

10 9 8 7 6 5 4 3 2 1

British Library Cataloguing in Publication Data available.

ISBN 1 84270 003 0

This book has been printed on acid-free paper

SCRAPS

MARK FOREMAN

Ⓐ

Andersen Press · London

Scraps was not like the others.

The elephant was all elephant. The kangaroo was all kangaroo.
The crocodile was all croc. The sailor was smart in his
sailor suit and the teds were all teds.

But Scraps was a bit of this and a bit of that. He was made from all the left-overs.

One day, Mrs Kelly, who had made all the animals during the past few weeks, put them all into a basket and took them off to market.

"Where are we going?" asked Scraps.
"To market, to market," said Big Ted.
"What's that?" asked Scraps.
"That's where children choose us and love us," said the crocodile.
"And take us home, don't forget that," said the elephant.

"I want to be taken over the sea," said the sailor.
"I want to go to the jungle," cried the monkey.
Scraps had no idea where he wanted to go. He rather liked it at
Mrs Kelly's.

It was very busy at the market.

"I love the elephant, Mum."
"I love the kangaroo . . . and the sailor."

One by one and sometimes two by two, the animals were sold

– all except for Scraps.

On the way home Scraps was very miserable.
"I'll be put back on the shelf," he sobbed. "All by myself."

"What are we going to do with you, little Scraps?" sighed
Mrs Kelly, when they arrived home.

"Stick him on the shelf until next market day," said Mr Kelly.
So, just as he feared, Scraps was put back on the shelf all by himself.

Mrs Kelly started knitting again.
"Good," thought Scraps. "She will make me some friends."
"But although Mrs Kelly knitted, no friends appeared. Instead she put all sorts of strange things into a drawer.

At night when the house was quiet, Scraps wondered where his old friends were now. Had the sailor gone over the sea? Was the monkey in the jungle? And what was it like to be loved?

In the daytime, Mrs Kelly knitted and sang, knitted and sang.
Everything she knitted went into the drawer.

Then, one day, Mrs Kelly came into the room carrying a baby. The baby was crying. Mrs Kelly sang, but the baby cried more. Mr Kelly sang but the baby still cried.

Mr Kelly sang and danced. Scraps laughed
so much he fell off the shelf, but the baby
cried even more.

Mr Kelly picked Scraps up off the floor and dangled him in front of the baby. As soon as the baby saw Scraps, the crying stopped. The baby smiled and hugged his new friend.

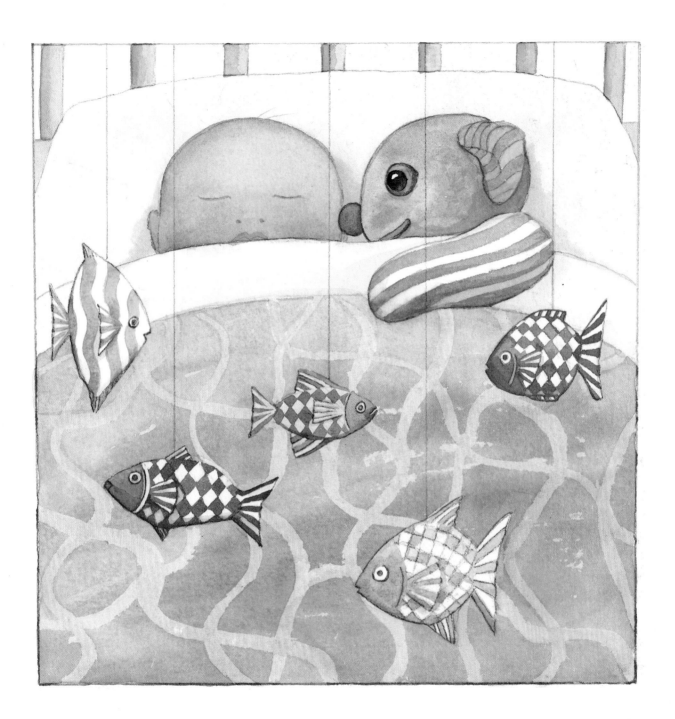

That night and every night, Scraps slept in the arms of the baby.
Next day and everyday, wherever the baby went, Scraps was sure
to go.

A few months later, Mrs Kelly began knitting animals again. Slowly the shelf filled up with teds, elephants, camels and crocodiles, ready

for market. But Scraps was never put on the shelf again.
He was loved already.

Make Your Own Scraps

Materials
Scraps of cotton fabric, Scraps of blue and red felt, Scraps of coloured wool, Needle and thread, Toy stuffing

Cutting out
On a piece of paper, draw a grid making each square 1 inch. Using the 1 cm grid as a guide, copy the pattern on to the sheet of paper with the 1 inch grid. Pin the pattern to fabric, remembering to use double thickness of fabric where indicated and cut. Transfer all pattern markings onto the fabric.

To make Scraps: allow 4 mm seam allowance throughout. RS = right sides.

EARS
Take two of the four pieces and with RS together, stitch from A to B to C. Repeat with remaining two pieces. Turn RS out and lightly stuff.
Take one sewn ear and pin to right side of head along XY so that seam is inserted into cut XY. Sew from X to Y through all four thicknesses of fabric. Repeat with other ear.

HEAD
With RS together sew up cheek darts. Match two head pieces, RS together and sew D to E to F. Open out head pieces and pin head gusset into head at D to A to G. Sew D to A to G on both sides. Gather around nose piece. Stuff and pull closed. Stitch onto RS of head at D. Sew up head dart, from To to G. Run a gathering stitch from F to G. Stuff head. Gather from F to G and sew.

BACK SPIKES
With RS together, sew two sides of spikes. Turn to RS. Lightly stuff.

TAIL
With RS together, sew round tail from A to B to C. Turn to RS. Lightly stuff.

ARMS
Sew paw to inside arm from A to B. With RS together, match inside arm to outside arm and sew from A to C to B to D, leaving a small hole for stuffing. Stuff arm firmly. Sew up opening. Repeat with other arm.

LEGS
Fold leg from A to C, RS together. Sew from A to B, leaving small opening for stuffing. Pin and sew foot pad on the bottom, matching B and C. Turn to RS. Stuff firmly. Sew up opening. Repeat for other leg.

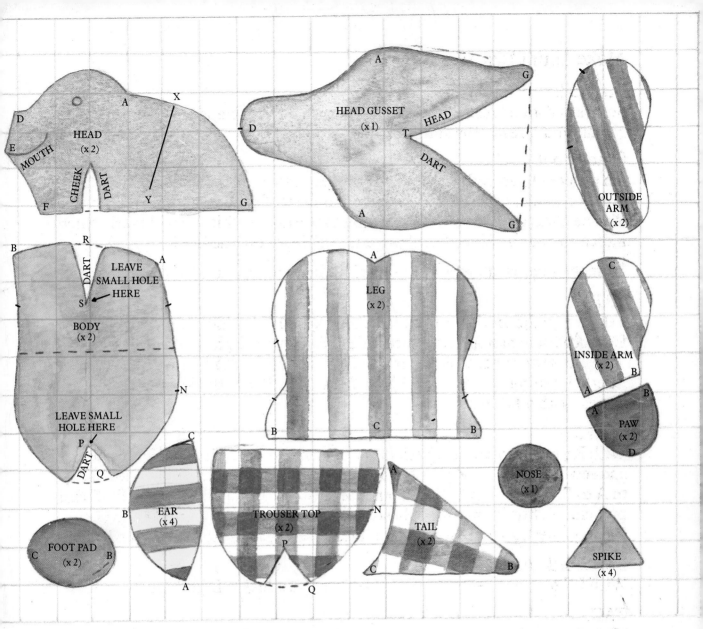

Pattern © 1990 Caroline Kelley

BODY

Pin trouser top to body and sew right round. Sew darts from R to S and from P to Q. Between the two RS, pin and tack tail on body back from N to Q and spikes to body back from A to N. Make sure that tail and spikes point inwards while you sew. With RS together, matching edges, sew up body from A to Q to B, sewing tail and spikes along A to Q. Turn right side out and stuff tightly. Gather from A to R to B and sew tightly.

Securely stitch arms and legs to body. Attach head by sewing tightly.

Using brightly coloured wool embroider eyes and mouth onto face.

More Andersen Press paperback picture books!

MICHAEL
by Tony Bradman and Tony Ross

THE SANDAL
by Tony Bradman and Philippe Dupasquier

OUR PUPPY'S HOLIDAY
by Ruth Brown

NOTHING BUT TROUBLE
by Gus Clarke

FRIGHTENED FRED
by Peta Coplans

THE PERFECT PET
by Peta Coplans

A SUNDAY WITH GRANDPA
by Philippe Dupasquier

I'LL TAKE YOU TO MRS COLE
by Nigel Gray and Michael Foreman

WHAT'S INSIDE?
by Satoshi Kitamura

THERE'S A HOLE IN MY BUCKET
by Ingrid and Dieter Schubert

A LITTLE BIT OF WINTER
by Paul Stuart and Chris Riddell

ELEPHANT AND CROCODILE
by Max Velthuijs